Silent Friends:

ANIMALS I HAVE KNOWN

~~~~~~~~~~~~~~~~~~ BY ~~~~~~~~~~~~~~~~~~

GENE HOOPES

Sketches by George Phippen

INKWELL BOOKS
Writing-Publishing-Printing

Silent Friends:

ANIMALS I HAVE KNOWN

~~~~~~~~~~~~~~~~~~~~ BY ~~~~~~~~~~~~~~~~~~~~

GENE HOOPES

Sketches by George Phippen

INKWELL BOOKS
Writing-Publishing-Printing

This book is published by Inkwell Books, under exclusive license from Beatrice Media, Inc.

First Inkwell Books printing: May 2014

ISBN: 978-1-939-625-02-1
Library of Congress Control Number: 2018912455

Published by Inkwell Books, LLC
10632 North Scottsdale Road, Unit 695
Scottsdale, AZ 85254
Tel. 480-315-3781
E-mail info@inkwellbooksllc.com
Website www.inkwellbooksllc.com

INKWELL BOOKS
Writing-Publishing-Printing

To

MY OWN GIPSY:

*she too a lover of our
silent friends*

NOTE

The following incidents all came under the writer's personal observation. They have been set down on these pages exactly as they happened, entirely without coloring or enlargement.

Two considerations have prompted this simple recording. First—that it might serve as a tribute, as it were, to the performers—all good friends of mine. Second—that others might thereby gain a better understanding of their silent friends of the animal world.

Dumb animals, they are commonly called. True, they do not speak the language we commonly use. But is that any proof that they are without intelligence?

G. H.

Contents

HORSES

DOGS

CATS

FOWLS

RANDOM SKETCHES

PETER THE GREAT

Horses

The faithful and uncomplaining
friend of man since the beginning of time,
giving so much, expecting so little in return

Billy the Magnificent

AS A LAD IN MY LATE TEENS I HAD A horse I called Billy the Magnificent. He was a magnificent animal, a golden sorrel with silver mane and tail. I was very proud of him, as well I could be, for he was a grand horse in every way.

Billy was a high-spirited animal, with definite ideas of his own. He had a wonderful disposition in the stable, but in harness one had to know how to handle him. That was my fault, perhaps; I had trained him, and probably spoiled him to some extent. Anyway, he resented having anyone else drive him, and for most of his days no one else attempted to drive him.

Those were the days before the automobile had come to usurp the roads, and driving a good horse was a real pleasure. Through our county there were many fine drives over the hard dirt roads. One of these went by a small ice-cream factory just beyond the town where I lived at that time.

One evening I had taken my girl friend for a drive, and on the way home we stopped for some ice cream. Billy never wanted to stop any place along the way, and if we did stop, he would impatiently paw the ground until we were off again. No road was too long for him, and he seemed to enjoy himself thoroughly.

Prompted by curiosity, I bought three dishes of ice cream that night and offered one to Billy. He sniffed it suspiciously before his own curiosity moved him to sample it. In those days, before the cone had been invented, ice cream was generally served on thin wooden dishes, with a wooden spoon.

One taste was enough for Billy—he liked it. When his teeth chilled, he would throw his head back and snort, but he cleaned up all the ice cream. And thereafter that was the only stop he had no objection to making. In fact, it was almost impossible to get him past the place. He would pay no attention to it on the way out, but it was not wise to try getting him past on the way home. He expected his treat, and of course, he always got it.

The factory only operated during the summer. When it was closed, Billy would trot past it as though it had not existed. How did he know it was not in operation? His sense of smell probably told him.

Billy liked tobacco also. I smoked stogies in those days. Billy grew to expect the privilege of clipping the end off one of them every time I went near him. He expected it from others also, and when he found someone who did not use tobacco, he had no more use for them. They failed to qualify, according to his notion of the fitness of things.

An Unintentional Mishap

WE WERE JOGGING ALONG A QUIET country road one evening, my girl friend and I, on our way home. We had just started down a hill when Billy shied at something on the road. Perhaps I was not paying too much attention to my driving at the moment, but be that as it may, we were quite unprepared.

I was using a light runabout at the time. The horse's sudden jump tipped the rig over, and the girl friend and I were deposited in the grass at the side of the road. Before I could get to my feet, the rig had settled back on four wheels, and William was going down the hill at a lively clip.

We were not hurt, so we gathered ourselves together, and started homeward. We had a three-mile walk ahead of us. I was not concerned about myself, but I feared the girl would fare badly in her high-heeled shoes. I felt certain that Billy would not stop until he had reached home. And I fully expected to find pieces of the rig scattered along the road. That was not a pleasant thing to contemplate, for the rig was comparatively new.

When we neared the bottom of the hill, I noticed a dark object just ahead of us. I hoped it might be the runabout, not too badly damaged. Imagine our amazement when we came close enough to see that it was not only the rig, but Billy as well. Failing to understand why there was no one behind him, the horse had kicked himself loose from the vehicle. When it had come to rest at the foot of the hill, he had returned to investigate. There he stood, patiently waiting for us to come and make things right again.

With a few quick repairs to the traces, we were again on our way home. The horse gave every evidence of being quite concerned about the mishap that he had unintentionally brought about.

Billy and the Doctor

I HAD A MARE THAT I DROVE WITH BILLY for a couple of years. They made a fine-looking team, but I finally had to let her go because of her mean disposition. She didn't like Billy. I am sure she was jealous of him because she knew he was her superior. He was endowed with more speed and more endurance. Moreover, he was much better-looking.

Well, the mare broke loose in the stable one night, and she took her spite out on Billy by kicking him when he could not defend himself. When I found them in the morning, Billy had an ugly gash on his hip about a foot long, and my feelings were not pleasant ones where that mare was concerned.

We had a veterinarian in the community, but I did not call him. I had seen him at work once, and I did not like the way he went about it. Instead, I called Perry Rockford, an old horseman whom I knew quite well. In my opinion, he knew more about horses than anyone in the county.

Rocker came—he had gotten that name because of his peculiar walk. He had known Billy for a long time, and had attended him for minor injuries several times. He went up to the horse and gave him a bite off his plug of tobacco. He stroked the glossy neck and cursed the mare in his own original way. While I was getting a bucket of hot water, Rocker had removed his coat and rolled up his sleeves.

I stopped him as he started to clean the wound. "Rocker," I said, "aren't you going to rope Billy?"

"What for?" he asked, going back to work.

"Why, man, he can kick your head off."

"You're right, son," he replied, smiling in his peculiar way. "He can, but he won't." Then addressing the horse, he said, "He doesn't know you yet, does he, old boy? I've always told him you had more sense than most folks he knows. You wouldn't kick me, because you and I are old friends. You know I wouldn't hurt you if I could help it. Now we'll show the kid something he ain't likely to forget in a hurry."

While he talked, Rocker finished cleaning the ugly wound. With head turned, Billy watched and listened. I took a long breath when Rocker ran a needle through the horse's flesh for the first stitch. Billy quivered slightly but made no move. Rocker continued to talk to the horse as though he had been an old crony.

It required fourteen stitches to close the wound. Rocker stood directly behind the horse as he worked, and never once did Billy offer the slightest protest. Yes, that was an exhibition of confidence between man and horse that I could never forget. It was indeed a good lesson for me.

A Worthy Competitor

THE COUNTY IN WHICH I LIVED DURING my youth was noted for its fine horses. Racing was not confined to the county fair; it was a year-round activity. The automobile was slowly capturing the public fancy, but these primitive vehicles were rarely seen during the winter months. The horse and sleigh still reigned.

One wide street in our town was set aside for the use of the racing fans. And when the sleighing was good, one could find the best horses in the county gathered there nightly to test their speed. The competition was keen, and it was great sport for horsemen and spectators alike.

The horse which I owned at that time had considerable speed, and great endurance. I think he enjoyed racing as much as I did, but he was not fast enough to go up against the top-notchers. Therefore, I imported a horse from the East one winter. This horse had been on the track for several years and had an excellent record. His name was Charlie Paddock, but we changed it to Charlie Madison.

Because of an injury, Charlie's racing days were thought to be over. That was why his owner had sent him to the winter auction at Madison Square Garden. There was certainly nothing in his appearance to warrant enthusiasm; hence I was able to pick him up at what soon proved a ridiculously low price. The injury had left him with an unsightly blemish, but it had not affected his speed to any extent.

The first heavy snow of the season had fallen the night of Charlie's arrival. I therefore hitched him to the sleigh the next day to see how he would perform in the snow. Very listlessly he jogged through the main street of our small town. His head hung on the check rein, and he appeared so tired that I did not have the heart to urge him. I could afford to wait until he had recovered from his tiresome trip in a boxcar. I did not have long to wait, however.

As we were nearing the end of the long street, I saw another sleigh approaching. Then I saw Charlie's head slowly lifting. His ears stiffened; his eyes gazed eagerly at the oncoming horse. Charlie Madison had suddenly come to life. I soon recognized the approaching horse. It was the fastest horse in the county, owned by one of my neighbors. For two years this fine animal had been undefeated in our friendly races.

I waved a greeting to my neighbor as we passed. I had allowed my horse to settle into an easy, ground-covering walk. Now his eyes were glued upon the horse on the other side of the street. His head turned to watch her as she trotted slowly by.

Then, without the slightest warning, he turned to follow. I was driving with a slack rein and had not even spoken to the horse.

Completing the turn, Charlie Madison immediately fell into a long, swinging trot. As we swiftly caught up, my neighbor glanced around. I may have been mistaken, but I thought the expression on his face was one of concern. Anyway, he quickly put his horse into a faster pace. Charlie promptly increased his speed also.

With no apparent effort on his part, and certainly no urging from me, we were soon going down that quiet street at top speed. Racing was not permitted on the main street, but I am sure neither of us gave a thought to that at the moment. My neighbor's reputation was at stake, and I was enjoying the situation too much to be mindful of what it might cost me. I was still driving with a light rein, letting Charlie Madison have his way. And it was quite evident that he was thoroughly enjoying himself.

The street widened to one hundred feet in the business section of the town, which was four blocks long. The swift jingle of bells emptied the stores that afternoon. A fair crowd of enthusiastic spectators cheered as we raced by, somewhat astounded perhaps at this flagrant violation of regulations.

Before we had left this wide section of the street, Charlie Madison had put the county champion well in the rear. And all I had done was sit back and smile my appreciation of this great horse that had fallen into my hands. Charlie Madison, in his wisdom, had quickly recognized a worthy competitor, and he could not resist the temptation to show his own wares that winter afternoon.

Bucky's Grief

OF ALL THE STRANGE AND INTERESTING experiences during the many years I have handled horses, this one takes first place. Even I might have had grave doubts concerning it had I not seen it myself. It proved—to me at least—that animals are capable of much deeper feeling than we are generally inclined to believe.

At the time of this incident Bucky and Lady were the top mounts on the ranch. Bucky had been with us several years. He was not old, but he had been in our service longer than any of the other horses. He was always the leader; no horse ever disputing that leadership for very long. He had never shown any favoritism until Lady came. The attachment between those two was nothing more nor less than love at first sight.

At first I thought Bucky had taken to the new horse merely because of her quality. She was one of the best horses we had ever owned, equal to Bucky in speed, and a good-looking animal. But the attachment was mutual and so genuine that I cast aside that theory.

Lady had been with us about two years when she took sick. The veterinarian was called immediately, but our efforts to save her proved futile. She died that night. Bucky had been around, of course, and knew that his ladylove was in trouble. And he had probably not been far from the corral all night. Of course, Lady had been shut up by herself. And when I went out in the morning to feed them, I knew from Bucky's attitude what I might expect. His pal was gone, and I never saw a more dejected-looking horse. He would not come into the corral for his breakfast, no, not even to get a drink. I took a bucket of water and some hay to him, but he would not touch either.

Lady was buried at the foot of a low hill that bordered the

pasture. Bucky, taking the other horses with him, went as far away as he could get; then for the balance of the day he stayed in that far corner of the field, alone. The other horses appeared indifferent regarding what had happened. But perhaps they understood Bucky's feelings and were considerately leaving him alone.

The pasture lay somewhat below the level of the house, and from there it was possible to see plainly the larger part of it. My wife and I were sitting on the porch that evening. Dusk was settling down upon the valley when Bucky's peculiar actions attracted our attention.

Some of the horses were grouped together as though discussing the events of the day—and who could say they were not? Others nibbled at the short grass. But Bucky's movements were quite different. Slowly but surely, he was drawing away from the others. It looked as though his desire was to get away from them without attracting attention. He would take a few steps, nibbling a bit of grass here and there, then stop. He would stand like a soldier at attention, so motionless that he looked like a statue. Then, with nose in the grass, he would move on.

By this time it was evident that Bucky had a definite objective, for he was moving straight toward the hill where Lady had been buried. When he finally came within a few yards of the grave, he stopped. This time he stood quite still for several minutes, head erect as though listening for something. And perhaps he was. We know that the animals have much keener senses than ours. They live much closer to Nature than we, so we have no way of knowing what may come to them from an invisible world.

Bucky may have heard the voice of his departed pal; we have no way of knowing. Be that as it may, however, after that period of listening he slowly approached the grave. There he stopped again, sniffing at the newly turned earth. And now, with his nose almost touching the ground, he stepped lightly around the grave. It was as though he were performing a sacred rite.

Having completed the circuit, he stopped. He stood there a long time, head erect and ears forward. Finally, with a sudden toss of his proud head, he trotted back to his companions.

We witnessed a repetition of that strange performance many times afterward. And there was never the slightest variation to it. The following morning I went to Lady's grave to have a look. To some extent, I thought, we might have been drawing upon our imagination. We had been watching from a considerable distance. Bucky's footprints left no room for doubt, however. He had circled the grave without once touching the fresh earth. Nor did he ever touch it afterward.

Often after he had performed this ceremony, he would come to the fence in front of the house. He would put his head over the gate and whinny. My wife would go down and talk to him. He had always been friendly enough, but never affectionate. But now he would put his head on my wife's shoulder and close his eyes while she consoled him. It was evident that he thought she understood, and he sought the comfort of her soft voice.

I had worked with this horse for years, and he knew I was his friend. Yet he never once came to me for consolation. In fact, he avoided me for weeks. He did not want me to touch him. It was clear enough that he considered me responsible for his trouble. When his pal had been stricken, he expected me to see that she got well again. Had I not taken care of him when he needed it? I had failed him in this case, and he showed his displeasure in no uncertain manner.

Waiting for Help

BUCKY WAS A NERVOUS, HIGH-SPIRITED animal that responded only to gentleness. A harsh word, or a quick movement unexpected, and he was almost unmanageable.

One afternoon I was on my way from the barn when I noticed Bucky standing not far from the house. Only his head was visible, and he was looking my way. When he saw me, he whinnied. I answered him, as I always did. He was alone, and so motionless that I became suspicious. I went to investigate.

We used barbed wire on the boundary fences, field-fencing around the house to keep the chickens out of the yard. Major had discovered that by putting his weight on the top of this fence and stretching his long neck, he could clip the stray weeds on the other side. The result was that the fence was sagged in several places. Hoping to stop this, a strand of barbed wire had been stretched along the top, but the clown was smart enough to keep his neck between the barbs. The only solution was to raise the fence a foot or two, but I had delayed doing it.

Major had undoubtedly paved the way for what had happened, for Bucky had great respect for barbed wire. He had been severely injured by it once, and he had not forgotten. Major had broken the fence and left Bucky to take the consequences.

He had both hind legs tangled in the wire. One would have expected a horse of his disposition to kick himself free, but Bucky had learned much from experience. He knew that I was not far off and that I would help him when I discovered his predicament. So he waited.

He was trembling as I went up to him, but he calmed down quickly when I spoke to him. One leg was freed without difficulty, but the other proved not so easy. The wire was firmly wedged under the heel of his shoe. I spoke to him again, explaining that I would have to get the wire cutters for that job. I stroked his neck, and he seemed to understand.

I was back in a couple of minutes, and Bucky had waited for me. I cut the wire, freeing his foot, but he did not move. I patted him again. "It's all right now, fellow," I told him. "No harm done." He shook his head knowingly and trotted off to join his pals. His patience, and his confidence in his master, had saved him another painful injury. Can anyone say that this was nothing but instinct?

Bucky Knows

IT MIGHT BE WELL TO EXPLAIN THAT this Bucky horse was not always the tractable animal that these sketches might indicate. We bought him when he was six years old, broken to the saddle, but by no means tamed. He was wild, and he was mean. He had probably never heard a kind word or known a gentle hand. He was suspicious of man and resented any effort to curb his freedom. I spent almost a year in convincing him that I was his friend, but after that there was no more trouble.

That friendship once established, the change that came over this horse was remarkable. He showed an intelligence that I had never suspected. He could even talk—in a limited way, of course. He talked with his ears and his eyes. If one knew him, it was nearly always possible to anticipate his intentions. His mental reactions found expression in the flick of an ear, a toss of his head, or the expression of his eyes.

Moreover, he acquired an amazing understanding of the language of man. It was a source of enjoyment, often amusement, to show him off to guests of the ranch. Most of them, no doubt, were never convinced that there was not some hokum about the things he would do.

There were many interesting places to go on our rides from the ranch. Each place had been named, and of course Bucky had heard those names many times. It was quite a while before I discovered that they had made any impression upon the horse; and then it was entirely by accident. I could hardly believe it myself, at first, but when I put him to the test, I was convinced. I kept this to myself until I was satisfied not only that he understood, but also that he was proud of his knowledge. He actually enjoyed demonstrating.

When I was getting him ready for a ride, I would tell him where we intended going. It had always been my habit to talk to the horses just as though they were human. I had learned that was the best way to get close to a horse. To get the best out of him by making him understand what was wanted of him. Not every horse will respond as Bucky did, of course.

Wife and I were riding alone one day when I let her in on the secret. She always rode Bucky, so it was impossible for me to have any control of him, even had I so desired. As we left the ranch, she asked me where we were going. I told her to give Bucky his head, he would take us to the place I had selected. I said I had told him we were going to the upper canyon and, if she would let him alone, I was sure he would take us there.

Now, there were several places along the route which Bucky liked as well, or even better, than the upper canyon, but that was where he took us. In my wife's opinion, Bucky was about

the smartest horse afoot, but this was almost unbelievable—
even for her. It required several demonstrations to convince her
that it was not mere coincidence.

Places many miles from the ranch could be selected—rough
going, often—but it made no difference to Bucky. Trails could
branch off to more favorable spots, short cuts back to the ranch
perhaps, yet he never hesitated. And when we had arrived at our
destination, he gave every evidence that he was quite pleased
with himself for having carried out our instructions.

Eventually I proved that it was necessary for Bucky to hear
the name of a place only two or three times. That was enough—
he knew, and he never once failed to prove that he knew. There
was only one place that he would not go of his own accord, and
that was to one of the neighboring ranches. He had taken a
dislike to that place the first time we were there, and he would
not go there if he could possibly avoid it.

A Fastidious Fellow

THIS BUCKY HORSE DEVELOPED A
characteristic which I have never seen equaled. It proved
decidedly useful to me, and I appreciated it. Perhaps it will
illustrate to what extent an intelligent animal will go in an effort
to co-operate with the master it loves.

When we took over the ranch, there was so much to be done
that many needed improvements had to be neglected. It was
quite a while before I could get around to building a box in
which to store the litter that accumulated in the corral. I always

tried to clean the place at least once each week. Several times I noticed that Bucky appeared quite interested in what I was doing. Until I could get the box built, I had been scraping the litter into a corner of the corral fence.

After a while I found that this chore was becoming lighter. So much so, in fact, that a cleaning once in two weeks was enough. Then I discovered the reason. The corner in which I had been storing the litter was being used for a toilet. Bucky was responsible for the new custom. And he was not only using it himself but was seeing to it that the other horses did likewise.

Undoubtedly Bucky had been doing some thinking as he watched me repeatedly scraping the dirt into that particular corner. If that was where I wanted it, he reasoned, he would do his best to help toward that end.

When Lady first came to us, her habits were very bad, but not for long. Bucky took her in hand, and it was amusing to watch him. When she would make a mess, perhaps right in front of the barn door, he would chase her into the corner toilet. It was not long before she was broken of her untidy habit. After that the only cleaning the corral required was an occasional collecting of trampled hay or weeds blown from adjacent fields. Otherwise cleaning was merely transferring the manure from the corner toilet to the storage box. No wonder Bucky stood so high in my esteem!

Nor was this fastidious habit confined to the corral. If possible, Bucky would always leave the trail when Nature demanded attention. He did the best he could to keep the trails clean. But here, of course, he had no influence upon the other horses. Bucky was quite a gentleman.

A Born Clown

we had acquired Bucky, and they were cronies for many years. Major was a big fellow, slow and deliberate in movement, but exceedingly wise. He was the one that would open the gates and turn on the water faucets every chance he had. Of course, he never bothered to close them.

He took great delight in kicking over a tub, or turning on the water, so that he could frolic in the mud. One had to be on guard when putting him across a stream. He never passed up an opportunity to lie down in the water. He gave me a couple of soakings before I got wise to him. As he would scramble out in response to the spur, it was plain to see that he enjoyed the joke, perhaps as much as he had enjoyed the refreshing dip.

One day we were training two of the horses for the "bending race." In this the rider guides his horse through a line of five-foot stakes, turning at the end and returning to the starting point. The stakes are not fastened to the ground. They stand on heavy bases and must not be touched during the race. The agility of a horse is more important than speed in this race.

We were working out in the pasture near the house, and being a curious animal, Major had ambled up to watch the performance. He had never seen anything like this before. As he watched us, his expression changed from interest to one that looked very much like disgust. Finally, as I put my horse over the course for the second time, Major suddenly whirled around and let both feet fly as we passed him. Now this was not like Major, and it puzzled me at first.

He trotted off a few yards, looking back at me rather sheepishly. He probably expected me to go after him, but I didn't. I only laughed and rode back to the starting line. Then that clown proceeded to demonstrate to us that he could play that game. Nonchalantly as could be, he trotted in and out of those stakes as though he had been doing it all his life. Completing the course without having touched a single stake, he went off down the field—laughing to himself no doubt.

A young chap from the East used to come to the ranch every summer. He was very fond of horses, but had much to learn about them. To him, Major was dumb but amusing. He had never ridden this horse on the trail, because, in his opinion, he had no spirit. But he did enjoy catching Major in the field or the corral and riding him bareback. Major was the only one of our horses that would permit anything of that nature.

We were on the front porch one evening when the lad decided to have a little fun with Major. The horses were grazing near the fence about a hundred yards away. Major shook hands with the lad, crunched a lump of sugar, and begged for more. Then the lad vaulted up on Major's back, facing the rear. The horse never moved, even when given a kick in the ribs. He only shook his head, as much as to say, "Not that way."

Then the lad began to inch up toward the horse's tail, until he was astride his hips. He looked up at us and waved. At that instant Major elevated his hind quarters just enough to toss the unwary rider to the ground. Then he raced down the field, kicking his heels in delight.

When the lad returned to the house, he expressed great surprise that Major had shown so much spirit. We told him that was because he did not understand the horse. Major was wise enough to conserve his energy for the proper occasion.

Peter the Psychic

AS SOON AS WE BECAME WELL SETTLED in our mountain home, we took time out to look for a couple of horses. The first one we took on was a beautiful golden sorrel, a big fellow, five years old. He bore the insignificant name Peanuts. We changed that name to Peter the Great, and we never had cause to regret the selection. Peter proved to be one of the greatest horses I had ever handled.

In a previous sketch we have told about the horse Bucky and his ability to remember the names of places. Peter had the same ability, perhaps not to the same degree, but he did not need it.

After I had been riding this horse for a year or so, I made a discovery. I am well aware that what I am about to relate will impress many readers as being so improbable that it borders on the ridiculous. Some may charge it to the writer's over-stimulated imagination. Unbelievable as it may seem, however, we are still dealing with fact only.

One of the churches had a large summer camp not far from where we lived. One of the main forest roads ran through these campgrounds. We had been over that road probably fifty times, or more, but we had never stopped at the camp.

I had met the caretaker several times, a very pleasant person. More than once he had suggested that we stop by some time when we were riding, but we had never done so.

We were on our way home from a ride one afternoon, taking the road which went through the camp. It was still rather early, and as we entered the camp grounds the thought came to me that this would be a good opportunity to call upon our new neighbors. My wife was following at some distance, so I did not attempt to transfer my thought to her.

The caretaker lived in one of three cabins built on a circle about a hundred yards back from the road. By the time we had reached the turnoff to these cabins I had not yet come to a definite decision as to whether we would make the call or not. The thought was still in my mind, but the decision was not mine.

Without the slightest hesitation, Peter left the road, walked up to the caretaker's cabin, and stopped. I stroked the proud neck, and said, "Why, Peter, I believe you're a mind reader."

Now to appreciate fully what the horse had done, several points must be kept in mind. First, we had never been in there before. Second, there was no visible inducement for the horse to explore the place, no grass which he might be permitted to clip. But above all that, I had not spoken a word to him or lifted a rein. The action was entirely voluntary on his part.

When we had reached home after our visit, my wife said to me, "You're a mind reader. As we were coming up the hill to the camp, I had the same thought about calling on those folks."

"No credit is due me," I told her. "Peter seems to be the mind reader. Anyway, he turned in there entirely of his own accord."

Of course, I thought afterward, it could have been a mere coincidence. Well, I was sure the question could be settled one way or another, and I set out to do just that. For some time afterward I took every opportunity to put Peter to the test. When we came to a fork in the trail I would merely give thought to the way I preferred. I would give no signal to the horse, nor speak a word, yet nine times out of ten he would take the trail I had in mind. I always praised him, and I am sure he was proud of his ability to please me.

It was not long before I was satisfied that this grand horse had the uncanny ability to sense my desires. He had a broad understanding of the spoken word, but he did not have to depend upon it.

A Unique Association

PETER THE GREAT WAS A HIGH-SPIRITED horse, sometimes quite a handful when under the saddle. It was always in the spirit of play, however, for there was certainly nothing mean about him at any time. In fact, he was as gentle as a kitten, with perfect manners. No matter where he might be, a call or a whistle would bring him trotting to the corral, ready for anything.

He was an exceedingly friendly horse, even with strangers. If strangers appeared at the corral, he would even leave the feed box and come to the fence to welcome them. He loved affection and seemed to care not whence it came. He was on very intimate terms with Gay, the cat.

Gay was a hunter, spending most of her time around the barn. She was quite small, but apparently had no fear of anything. Often when I would be getting Peter ready for a ride, she would show her attachment for him by rubbing up against his legs, purring her contentment the while.

If Peter lowered his head, Gay would rub his nose. Then Peter would catch her fluffy tail in his lips and very gently lift her hindquarters off the ground. There was never any protest from the cat. When released, she would just shake herself and come back for more. It was quite evident that there was a complete understanding between these two extremes of the animal world. It was an object lesson in good will.

Self-appointed Guardian

AFTER ACQUIRING PETER THE GREAT, WE tried out several horses, but none proved satisfactory. Finally, we found a young mare that looked very promising. Sandra was her name, and Peter took to her at once. In fact, the attachment quickly became mutual.

The corral was at the foot of a low hill a considerable distance from the house. Winter in the mountains was usually rather rugged. Therefore, as soon as the weather broke in the fall, we sent the horses to town.

We were surprised and decidedly annoyed to discover the following summer that Sandra was going to have a baby. Something had gone amiss during the winter, and no one seemed to know anything about it. This presented an unpleasant situation. Undoubtedly it would be a troubled one, at least, until we could dispose of the colt.

Peter and Sandra had gotten along beautifully, but no one could predict what the arrival of the colt might do to that relationship. Peter had a jealous disposition, and we could not picture him quietly accepting an intruder. I was certain that we would have to keep them separated, and that would make Peter most unhappy. He was positively miserable if he had to be alone.

Soon after the arrival of the colt, however, we found that our fears had been entirely unnecessary. When the colt was about two weeks old, we went to town one day to see how she was getting along. Much to our surprise, neither the horses nor the colt were in the barn where they belonged. We found them all together in an adjoining lot. This was contrary to our instructions.

It was quite plain, however, that we had no need for concern. Peace and harmony prevailed. Even our attentions to the colt failed to produce the expected reaction from Peter. Prompted by curiosity, no doubt, a couple of strange horses came up to the fence near by. Peter, with ears back and teeth bared, promptly drove them off.

That show of proprietorship quickly put my mind at ease. Peter was as proud of that colt as though it had been his very own. He now had two girls to look after, and he had assumed his responsibility with unmistakable pride. And it was not long before it was quite evident that the colt was as fond of Peter as she was of her mother, perhaps even more so. That was not strange, however. Sandra was a very sedate animal, while Peter was just the opposite. He was always ready to play with the baby, and they surely had a good time together.

Peter was exceedingly tolerant with his charge, yet he did not always approve of her conduct. We were quite amused one day at the way he reproved her. We always took the colt with us when we rode, and she had a grand time romping through the woods at will. She had formed a teasing habit of slipping up beside us and nipping at my pants or at Peter. On this particular day she had evidently thought up a new trick. Instead of nipping at us, she suddenly rose on her hind legs and tried to encircle Peter's neck with her forelegs.

Peter shied away from her embrace and stopped. The colt, chuckling to herself perhaps, went to munching a clump of grass. Peter immediately stepped up beside her. There they stood for a full minute, with their heads close together. There was no sound, of course, but something must have passed between them. Finally Peter raised a foreleg and brought it down again with marked force, as much as to say, "Now, young lady, don't do that again." And strangely enough, the colt never again attempted that trick.

Undoubtedly the colt had understood Peter. Moreover, she manifested due respect for the authority of her fond guardian.

A Wise Baby

THE COLT THAT PETER HAD ADOPTED was a lovable bundle of good spirits with a wonderful disposition. She was exceedingly affectionate and had no fear of anything.

When she was about four months old, she injured a hind leg. It had probably happened during one of her frolics with Peter. For quite a while it was necessary to bathe the leg several times a day in hot water, and to keep it bandaged. She was halterbroken, but it was never necessary to tie her. After the first treatment she seemed to understand what it was all about, and would stand quietly until it was all over. Her co-operation made my task decidedly easier. She did pull the bandage off during the first night, but never afterward.

She had hardly recovered from that injury when she ran into something one day, tearing an ugly gash in her face. This was beyond my first-aid facilities, so the doctor was called. He fully expected the colt to give us trouble when the needle was run through her sore flesh, but she never flinched. She stood like a soldier while the doctor put four stitches in her face. All I did was stand by and gently rub her ears and talk to her.

When the doctor had finished, she rubbed her nose against his face, as much as to say, "Thank you, doctor."

The wound was healing nicely when she somehow pulled out two of the stitches. Again the doctor was summoned. Since we could never be certain of the time of his arrival, I saddled the horses for a ride. Lest he come during our absence, we did not go far. We met him on the road. The colt was with us, of course.

And right there on the road, without being tied, her wound was cleaned and dressed. She nosed the doctor to show her gratitude, then trotted off to nibble some grass close by. She was only a baby, yet she had given proof of unusual intelligence and understanding. She also showed a rare gift of appreciation.

A Sad Break

THE FIRST UNFORTUNATE BREAK IN OUR happy family came when Peter the Great was suddenly called to his reward. He had been with us for nearly four years, and his going left us sad indeed. We could not expect to ever replace this faithful and loyal friend.

The whole place was plunged into gloom. Tippy, our dog, was never so happy as when escorting us on our rides. He was very fond of Peter, and his grief over the loss of his friend was unmistakable. That was also true of Gay, the little cat that had attached herself to Peter. They gave evidence of their grief in no uncertain way.

The colt was nine months old at this time. Her grief, and that of her mother, was something to touch the most hardened observer. They lost interest in food, spending much of their time pacing the corral, watching and listening, no doubt, for the return of their idol. They acted as though they were completely lost without him.

To eliminate the necessity of sending the horses to town again, we had built a new barn that summer. It was located closer to the house. During bad weather we could keep the horses there where it would not be difficult to care for them. As soon as Peter was gone, we moved Sandra and the colt to these new quarters. We hoped the new environment might be a help to them at this time, but it was not.

It had been several years since my wife and I had been away from home for more than a day. Now, since the place was so forlorn without Peter, it seemed a good time to get away. Being fortunate enough to get a reliable man to look after things for us, we took off on a week's vacation.

When we returned we were informed that everything had been quiet and peaceful during our absence. When I went to the corral that evening, I was pleased to see that the horses seemed to be taking a little more interest in their rations. But their discontent was still evident.

It was a long-established custom of mine to visit the corral before retiring. I wanted to be sure that the horses had plenty of water and that all was well with them. When I went to the corral this first night after our return, it was to find that there were no horses there. Investigation revealed a break in the fence. Sandra and the colt were gone. I called and whistled, but there was no answer. It would be useless to look for them before morning.

So, leaving the corral gate open, I returned to the house. I was certain the horses would be back by feeding time in the morning. They had gotten out many times before, but had always returned in a short while. I was undressing when it occurred to me that when they did come back it would hardly be to the new quarters. No, they would surely go to the old corral, and I had better open that gate before I turned in.

Perhaps I was about thirty yards from the old corral when I saw the dim outline of the colt standing at the gate. I called, and she came trotting up the path to meet me. By the time I had opened the gate Sandra came from behind the barn. I put some hay in the rack, but they did not touch it. They were busily investigating every corner of the corral. Unquestionably they were looking for their old pal.

The horses had been in their new quarters for two weeks, making no effort to escape; they broke out the first night after we returned from our trip. There is plenty of good grazing in the woods, but they had no interest in it. Their one desire was to be back in the old corral. Why? Well, it will probably sound very silly to some, but this is my firm belief. In my humble opinion there is only one logical answer.

When Sandra and the colt saw us coming in that afternoon,

they thought we might have brought Peter back with us. If we had, we must have left him down at the old corral. And they could not rest until they had satisfied themselves. It would be difficult indeed for anyone to convince me that a horse does not possess the power of reason.

A few days later, we took another horse on trial, hoping it might tend to relieve the loneliness in the corral. He was a good horse, with a grand disposition, but the experiment was a failure.

Sandra had always been so meek and so docile, but now she was positively fiendish. The colt showed a disposition to be friendly with the newcomer, but not Sandra. She would have none of him, so we had to send him back. Sandra was not accepting a substitute for her departed lover. Knowing Peter the Great as we did, and her love for him, we could not blame her. She preferred to live with her grief.

Dogs

A dog will gladly
give his life for his master.
Where can a greater love be found?

Mike Flannigan

WE HAD NAMED HIM MIKE. ONE OF OUR guests, an Irishman, of course, had added the Flannigan. Mike was a great favorite with the guests of the ranch, and he became known from coast to coast. It was a rare thing to receive a letter, from anyone who knew him, without a query concerning Mike.

Ever since we had taken over the ranch I had wanted a dog, but not just any kind of dog. A bull terrier was my choice, with no support from the other side of the house. I knew, however, from the discussions of the subject that my partner was not familiar with the type of dog I had in mind.

One winter night I went to the pump house to close the ventilators. This structure also housed the electric-light plant. It was customary to close it during cold weather just before we retired. I had just opened the door that night when a dog suddenly appeared out of the darkness.

He came up to me with tail wagging and a friendly sparkle in his big brown eyes. I put my hand on his broad head and spoke to him. "Hello, fellow," I said. "Where did you come from?" He was unable to answer my question, of course, but he gave ample evidence that he was glad to see me.

He followed me into the pump house, and I switched on a light to have a better look at the stranger. He was a big fellow, weighing about fifty pounds, with trim legs and full chest. He was not a tramp, being too well fed for that. I had never seen him before. I thought he may have been dropped from a car that had gone through the valley. Strange cars were somewhat rare, however, as we were twenty miles from the main highway. My theory did not appear too sound.

The stranger needed no urging to follow me to the house. When I opened the kitchen door, instead of rushing in as most dogs would have done, he stood there looking up at me anxiously. Well trained, I thought, but I was to learn that he had known almost no training. He was a gentleman by instinct. He made no move until I invited him in.

The wife was sitting by the open fire in the living room. Without any hesitation the dog went to her and put his head in her lap. There were exclamations of delight on her part as she stroked the glossy head. Mike had sold himself. She could hardly believe it when I told her that he was a fine specimen of my kind of dog. His color was a gray and tan brindle with four white feet, a white tip on his tail, snow-white collar and vest.

In a few minutes Mike had settled himself before the fire, and with a sigh of contentment was soon asleep. Now, what were we going to do with him was the question. Keep him, of course, I urged. But he might belong to a neighboring ranch, and we had no right to coax him away. But no coaxing was required. Mike had made himself at home, showing no inclination to leave.

It was nearly a week before we found out where he had come from. He belonged to the new owners of an adjoining ranch. That was why we had not seen him. Inasmuch as they had another dog, we had no difficulty in acquiring Mike.

These people had taken Mike when he was a puppy. The

older dog was the favorite, of course, being allowed into the house and granted all privileges. Mike had not been so favored, and he resented it. He grew tired of playing second to his inferior—and the other dog was inferior. So Mike had decided to find himself a home where he would be appreciated. He knew he was worthy of a better environment, as indeed he proved himself to be.

Never but once did Mike return to his former home, and that was strictly a business visit. It had evidently taken him several weeks to be satisfied that he had made himself solid with us. Then he went back to even the score with his former companion. For a time it looked as though the other dog would never recover from the battle, but he did. Mike, however, never so much as looked at him afterwards. That was only one of many instances in which Mike demonstrated his ability to do his own thinking.

Mike on Guard

THE BROWNS WERE SPENDING A MONTH at the ranch one spring. The weather had been wonderful, and toward the end of their stay Mrs. Brown expressed a desire to spend a night in the open. No men were wanted; it was to be an outing for women only.

The campsite selected was a rock-strewn mesa some five miles from the ranch. Since it was only half a mile from a road, they could take the car close to where they would make camp. They did not want to be bothered with horses.

As the car was being packed, Mike took his place back of

the seat. He did not often express a desire to go with us in the car. He loved to go with the horses but cared little about the car. I wondered if he intended going with the women or had merely been prompted to see what was going on.

Mike was still in the car, however, when my wife and Mrs. Brown left right after supper. They planned to have breakfast in the open and be back before noon next day. Mr. Brown was certain that Mike would not stay with the women, but I did not share his opinion. Although this would be a new experience for him, I was certain Mike would never desert his mistress. He knew the women were going to be alone, and he considered it his duty to go along to protect them. It proved that such must have been his reasoning.

We were given the story when the women returned the next morning. While it was being told, Mike slept as though he had been on an all-day trip with the horses. This was the story.

The moon had risen by the time the campers had arranged their bedrolls and prepared for the night. During this time Mike had made a careful inspection of the immediate territory, smelling each rock and investigating each bush. His blanket had been taken along, and it was spread between the two beds. But Mike had no use for it. He selected the highest spot near the camp, about fifty feet away. From this point he had an excellent view for a considerable distance in every direction.

No amount of persuasion would induce Mike to leave the spot he had chosen. My wife was a light sleeper, and she said she had wakened a dozen times during the night. Mike had always been in the same place, as far as she knew. And always sitting up. He sat there all through the night, listening, watching. The coyotes howled not far off, but there was never a sound out of Mike. He was as silent as a sphinx.

Mike never barked unless, in his opinion, something made it worth while. If the coyotes ventured closer to the ranch than he thought they should, he would warn them; otherwise he was always very quiet. This night the coyotes had come close enough for him to let them know he was on the job, but he did not bark. He evidently felt it would not be wise; to do so would be to betray the location of his charges.

Until the dawn broke over the eastern ranges, Mike kept his vigil. Then, deeming the danger to have passed, he came and stretched out on his blanket. There he slept until breakfast was ready. Had Mike not thought it all out for himself, and planned his course of action accordingly? The evidence certainly pointed strongly in that direction.

Mike Remembers

IT WAS INTERESTING TO WATCH MIKE'S reactions on our trip north one summer. When the war put the quietus on the guest business, we decided to see what the state of Oregon had to offer. As stated before, Mike did not care much for the car. The longest trip he had ever taken was to town once when he had to spend a few days in the hospital.

We traveled in a coupé which had a large compartment back of the seat. Mike's blanket was put on top of this compartment, and he was told that was where he must stay. He had a clear view in all directions, and was apparently quite satisfied. He seemed to understand fully that we were leaving the home he loved so well. With troubled eyes, he had watched the packing for days. When all was ready, he took his place in the car, but with an utterly dejected air.

It was quite evident that, in his opinion, there was no sense in leaving such a good home. Much to our surprise, however, he proved a wonderful traveler, never restless, but sleeping most of the time. When we stopped, he was out immediately to attend to his needs, but always ready to be off again.

Our home in Oregon did not please Mike at all. It was on the edge of a forest where there was plenty of room for him to roam, but he did not like it. Perhaps his discontent was largely because there were no horses. And there were no stray cows to keep off the place. He was lost.

Mike was certainly an unhappy dog, that year we spent in Oregon. He was pleased when we left, yet not too enthusiastic. He probably looked forward to landing in another distasteful location. On the way south he behaved about as he had going up, quite indifferent—until we crossed the Colorado river. Then he pricked up his ears and became interested. The country from Navajo Bridge to Flagstaff is not unlike much of what he had seen in eastern Oregon and southern Utah. But Mike saw a difference, or perhaps he smelled it.

Be that as it may, he was his old self from then on. As we came up the hill from the bridge, I nudged my wife. Mike was close against my back with his head out the window, sniffing. There was a new light in his expressive eyes. Undoubtedly he knew he was on the way home again—even though home was still some two hundred miles away.

Perhaps the brightest spot in Mike's enforced stay in Oregon was, strangely enough, a cat. Like most of his kind, Mike had little liking for that tribe. At the ranch he had merely tolerated the cats; he was never mean to them but never friendly.

One morning late in the winter a kitten wandered into our place, but Mike escorted him out in short order. Next morning the kitten was back again, and once more Mike sent him flying. But that kitten was not easily discouraged; he came back the third time. He seemed to have taken a liking to our place. This time he refused to leave, taking refuge in a tree near the house. We needed a cat, and I hoped this fellow might win out; but I did not think his chances were very favorable.

From a position where I could not be easily seen, I watched the outcome. I felt certain Mike would kill the kitten if he could, and I intended to prevent that if possible. The kitten was in the tree for fully half an hour, watching Mike on the lawn below. Finally Mike withdrew to a little distance from the tree and stretched out on the grass, with apparent indifference. I took this to be merely a ruse on his part.

Anyway, the kitten came slowly down from his place of safety. Reaching the ground, he calmly walked over to where Mike was lying. It looked as if it were time I took a hand in the affair before it was too late. The kitten was only a few feet from Mike when I reached him. He seemed quite unconcerned. He looked up at me with a pathetic greeting. Mike just wagged his tail, making no move.

Taking the kitten to the kitchen door, I got him a pan of milk. Mike watched the stranger lap up the milk, and I watched Mike. The kitten was about half grown, poor and distressed-looking. It seemed half starved. When he had cleaned up the last drop of milk, he took his seat beside Mike and proceeded to wash his face. Concluding that that cat could take care of himself, I went about my own affairs.

Muggins, as we named him, had somehow sold himself to Mike. And this time it was not a matter of tolerating the cat so far as Mike was concerned. They became great friends, even to the point of eating together. Was it because Mike respected the kitten's courage and persistence? Or had he found out in some mysterious way that Muggins too had known the misery of an unhappy home, and had set out to find himself a better one? Did Mike remember his own experience and extend his sympathy to this forlorn kitten? We shall never know, but we do know that there was an understanding between them. We also know that Muggins was a grand cat, decidedly happy and contented with his new home. And we were grateful to Mike for having so graciously accepted the little fellow.

Mike's Piety

MIKE KNEW VERY FEW TRICKS, AS SUCH. He was two years old when he came to us, and his former owner had not troubled to teach him anything.

He had an assortment of his own, of course—ways of expressing himself, for the most part. Should he be the subject of an unpleasant discussion, he could yawn most effectively. It was as though he said, "Oh, heck, let's change the subject." He could also sneeze at will and often employed that in an effort to get himself out of difficulties.

We did teach him to sit up, shake hands, and say his prayers. This latter, however, actually required no training; it seemed to come to him quite naturally. He was usually rewarded with something he liked when he had said his prayers. But that was not the only use he made of prayer. And no one could observe him at such times without being impressed by the manner in which he did it.

He would often say his prayers voluntarily, to express his gratitude or his sympathy when something had gone amiss. For example, if he knew his mistress was troubled about something, he would sit up and put his paws on her lap. Then, with an expression of deepest devotion, he would drop his head between his paws and close his eyes. It was as though he said, "I understand."

Saying his prayers, at times like that, was not a trick with Mike. There was something very real about it then, and he expected no reward. His piety was real when it was called for.

Jenny Takes Over

IT COULD BE ARGUED THAT THE incidents relative to Mike Flannigan were no proof of intelligence in dogs generally. Perhaps not, but surely they prove that the capacity to think does exist. And other incidents will be cited to show that Mike was not alone in this development.

Long before Mike's time I had owned a female bull terrier named Jenny. She had nine puppies in her first litter and raised them all without difficulty. As soon as they were, in her opinion, old enough, she started their training. Each morning she would put them through their paces, one at a time. She was teaching them the art of battle, as she knew it.

Jenny had never been in the fighting pit, but she had come from a long line of champions. The fighting game was instinctive with her. It was highly amusing to watch her train those youngsters in the tricks of the game. For the most part, they were by no means enthusiastic; they knew of better ways to amuse themselves. But there was no escape. She would tease them until they became angry; then she would demonstrate the ways of warding off their attacks upon her. After the lessons she would romp with them to show that it had all been in fun.

The puppies in this litter were all sold except one female. She was a nice pup, but a bit flighty. She had been named Muddle because she never seemed quite certain of anything. In time she too brought forth a family. The puppies were two days old when I was informed one evening that I had better take a look at them.

Muddle had made her bed in the hayloft, and I had seen them that morning. They were quite all right then. Muddle met me at the head of the steps in evident distress. I hardly knew what to expect when I went to look at the babies, certainly not what I found there. The puppies were all there and as busy as could be—getting their supper from their grandmother.

Muddle looked at them and whined, only to be driven off by her own mother. She made several timid attempts to assert her rights but finally gave it up. Jenny took complete charge of those puppies, raising them according to her own ideas. She was able to nurse them because she had just weaned her second litter a few days before.

It was evident, to me at least, that Jenny did not consider her daughter capable of bringing up a family. Anyway, not according to her standards, and in that she was right.

At another time Jenny gave evidence of her understanding, quite fortunately for us. The dog was with us in the den one evening. This room was on the second floor just above the kitchen. Junior, then three years of age, had been romping with Jenny. My wife had left the room to answer the telephone.

Jenny, tiring of the play, had slipped out of the room when Junior was not watching her. I had noticed that, but failed to observe that Junior had followed soon afterward. After a while

I heard Jenny whining insistently down in the kitchen. Knowing that something was amiss, I went to investigate.

Jenny was stretched out upon the kitchen floor with her nose against the door. Junior, our angel child, was sitting on the dog's back industriously chewing her ears. Jenny understood that the baby knew no better. She had not barked, not even growled—lest she frighten him, perhaps.

She could easily have shaken him off, of course. But he might have been hurt, had she done that. Jenny loved babies. She had merely whined, calling for help in the only way she knew.

Jenny the Faithful

JENNY, MATED TO PRINCE, ONE OF THE finest dogs I had ever owned, had reared four litters of puppies. Having had some difficulty in disposing of the last lot, I decided not to breed her again. So, when she was in heat again, I sent her away. Knowing there would be considerable annoyance under the circumstances, this seemed the best way to avoid it. The man who worked for me took her to his place, with orders to lock her in the basement. Jenny came home, however, several days earlier than she should. Someone had forgotten to secure the cellar door, and she had escaped.

It was a Sunday afternoon when she came home. The timing was unfortunate, for we were on the front porch with some friends. I heard a commotion out on the street but, being unable to see what it might be, gave it no thought. But as the noise grew louder I became suspicious. Our house was a considerable distance from the street.

My suspicion was confirmed when I saw Jenny round a curve in the driveway, leading a large procession. At her heels were at least twenty dogs, of all sizes and descriptions. They paraded by with a loud clatter, Jenny never looking our way. At such a time one has a great desire to be alone.

Excusing myself, I went to drive off the ambitious rabble and lock Mistress Jenny in the barn. Afterward, however, I decided that such loyalty should not go unrewarded. That dog had traveled more than a mile, fighting off her admirers, to come home to her mate. It was a wonderful example of fidelity.

Jenny Avenges Herself

THE PUPPIES IN THAT LAST LITTER were about half grown when the tragedy occurred. There had been many opportunities to breed Prince to strange dogs, but I had never even considered it. It was a friend who finally prevailed upon me. He had a very fine female of the same breed, and he was so insistent that I finally agreed to the mating.

Not caring to send Prince away, we arranged that my friend would bring his dog to our place. That proved to be a fatal mistake on my part. Twenty-four hours after my friend had taken his dog home Prince was dead.

Jenny, with the help of her sharp-toothed and well-trained brood, had put an end to her mate. She had cunningly chosen a time when there was no one near to interfere with her designs.

The battle was still in progress when they were finally discovered —but it was much too late.

While Jenny was doing the heavy work in the battle, those pups were literally stripping the hide off their father. There was nothing to do but put the poor fellow to sleep. He would have bled to death in a short time.

Jenny had proved her loyalty to her mate. She did not know that his dereliction should not have been charged to him. It was not her disposition to tolerate any unfaithfulness on his part. She expected as much from him as she had given. And she knew no other way to avenge herself.

Tippy's Answer

THE WINTER OF 1948–49 WAS AN unusually severe one. During January it looked as though it would never stop snowing, and for weeks at a time we were unable to reach the highway. Had trouble developed during those periods, we would have been in a bad way, with no near neighbors and no telephone.

It was a rather rugged experience, for we were not yet prepared for that sort of weather. We therefore decided to move into town the following winter. This one proved to be quite mild, permitting us to make frequent trips out to our mountain home.

If it was not too cold, we would often take a lunch with us and picnic in front of the big fireplace in the living room. We

always took our dog Tippy with us, and these occasions were a great delight to him.

When Tippy came to us, he was about three years old. He had been with us only a year, but he had given ample proof of unusual intelligence. It took one of those excursions to the country, however, to show us the depth of his understanding.

Tippy loved his home in the mountains, where he could roam at will. He did his best to reconcile himself to town life, but it was plainly evident that he was not contented. One day, after lunch, we sat before the fire for quite a while discussing ways and means of making the place more livable in winter. When we were about to leave, my wife put an arm about Tippy's neck and said, "Don't you wish we could come home to stay, Tippy? I sure do."

The dog wagged his tail, as though in full sympathy with the desire of his mistress. It was not until the following day, however, that we discovered how well Tippy had understood, and how anxious he was that we should know just how he felt in the matter.

We had been invited to spend that evening with some friends. Tippy was not at home to greet us when we returned. There was a tight wire fence all around the place, and he had never attempted to make his escape from this unaccustomed confinement. But tonight he had dug his way out. Morning came and Tippy had not come back. My wife expressed the belief that he had gone back to the country. I did not think so, for I could not imagine him leaving us for that length of time.

Nevertheless, we drove out to the country immediately after breakfast. And much to our relief, Tippy was there to welcome us home. He had traveled nearly seven miles over strange streets and through the dark forest to give us his answer. It was the only way he knew to tell us that he was in full accord with our desires.

Sensing Trouble

THE DEPTH OF AN INTELLIGENT animal's understanding is often quite amazing. We may find it so, at least, if we will only take the trouble to give it due consideration.

Our dog Tippy furnished an excellent illustration of this one time. It was an unusually fine day in the late fall. So, with no urgent call upon our time, my wife and I elected to take a drive. Of course, Tippy was delighted to be included in the excursion.

We were cruising on a narrow dirt road along the side of a mountain when a heavily loaded truck came roaring around a sharp curve. It was so sudden and so unexpected that there was no time to think. Fortunately we had been moving very slowly. We were on the outside of the road, with a decidedly uninviting drop facing us. I could only guess as to how close to the edge we might be and hope for the best. The driver of the truck scraped the hillside, and somehow we missed each other.

It had been an uncomfortably narrow escape. My wife was by no means a timid person. In fact, I had never seen her really frightened. This experience, however, had shattered that long record. She was decidedly upset. And in a very short while afterward Tippy began to act in a most unusual manner.

He started by sniffing at his mistress, her hands and arms, rubbing his nose against her face and neck. Then he would transfer his attention to me, rubbing his head against my arm and looking up at me with pleading eyes. Failing to get a satisfactory response, he would get in back of me, rubbing his nose on my neck. Not content with that, he would try to push my hat off or to nip at my ear.

This was such an unusual performance that we were at a

loss to understand it. Tippy was an instinctive gentleman, rarely ever touching one with his tongue or nose as most dogs will. At first I thought he might be coaxing for a hike in the woods.

No, that could hardly be the answer. The dog was unmistakably troubled. That was evident in his expressive eyes. It was impossible to quiet him. He kept up this strange performance until we had gotten off that rather dangerous road. Then, with a last sniff at his mistress, he lay down and was quiet for the rest of the trip.

Well, it finally dawned upon our fancied intelligence. Tippy had never before known his mistress to be frightened, and it had distressed him. His nose had told him of the fear that had shaken her, and he was doing his best to impress me with his concern. He expected me to do something about it.

Cats

So often misunderstood,
so useful to our civilization

Puff the Emotional

opinion of the cat family. I did not dislike them; they just failed to appeal to me. They had their place in the general scheme of things, of course, but I had not observed that they had any particular intelligence. But time proved that was only because I had not troubled to get acquainted with this branch of the animal world.

A better understanding of the cat family began with an Angora kitten. He had been given to us when we went on the ranch. He looked like a golden puffball, so we named him Puff. He was a cute little fellow and plenty smart. It had been agreed that he would not be permitted into the house. In my opinion, a house cat was an abomination.

Puff took care of his duties about the barn in a satisfactory manner, and I came to think quite well of him. When he was about a year old, one of the horses stepped on him, and the result was a broken leg and a broken tail. For a time it looked as though he might not recover, for he had also been injured internally. For months he could scarcely walk, even after his leg healed. He ate barely enough to keep him alive.

It soon became evident that his suffering was also mental. He had lost part of his gorgeous tail, and he seemed to realize that his beauty was forever marred. He was so pathetic that I made a special effort to console him. It was in the summer, and when we would be on the porch in the evening, I would take him in my lap.

I talked to that cat just as though he had been a close friend. And I feel certain that he came to understand much that I said to him. Anyway, it was not long before my interest in him began to yield results. His attitude changed; he grew less sensitive about his bobbed tail. However, I doubt if he ever became entirely reconciled to that loss. But his appetite gradually improved and he became playful, also very talkative. He never went to anyone else for consolation. He accepted me as his friend; the others were merely incidental. And so it always was.

When winter came, Puff was well on his way to complete recovery. And when it was no longer possible to have our evening chat on the porch, I put up a plea that he be allowed in the house. The concession was granted—for the evenings only.

If I happened to be busy at something when Puff came into the living room, he would go to my favorite chair and inform me in no uncertain manner that it was time for us to get together. He never offered to get into the chair until I had taken my place. If I were reading the paper, he would crawl under it or try to pull it out of my hand.

I noticed that he was demanding less attention as he grew stronger. After a few minutes of play, he would leave me and stretch out in front of the fire. There were two leather-covered cushions by the fireside. One evening Puff decided to appropriate one of them for his own use. This met with protest from the mistress of the house, but again I championed Puff's cause. I argued that he could not hurt the leather, and everyone else in the family had a seat of his own. And again I won.

I tried to explain to Puff that he must not take advantage of the privilege that had been given him. I have no way of knowing, of course, that he understood. I only know that he never attempted to extend the privilege.

One evening when Puff had finished his visit with me, he discovered that someone was sitting on his cushion. He could have taken the other cushion, but he didn't. He voiced his displeasure, mildly at first but with rising temper when the seat was not vacated. Strangely enough, he did not appeal to me for help. Seeming to realize that I was not the boss of the household, he went to my wife.

In a voice to touch the most hardened, he did his best to tell her his troubles. She advised him to take the other cushion, but he was not interested. Finally that cat actually shed tears. They rolled down his cheeks in the most pathetic way imaginable. That settled it; he got his cushion immediately. And proving that it had not been a mere coincidence, the same performance was repeated several times afterwards. Puff could certainly turn on the pathos when the occasion demanded.

Betty Moves In

WE CERTAINLY HAD NO NEED OF another cat when Betty moved in. Puff was back on the job again, and although not overly ambitious, he was doing well enough. Betty was a calico cat, hardly full grown when she appeared at the kitchen door one spring morning.

We found out later that she had belonged to our nearest

neighbor. These people had moved a few days before. And, as is so often the case, they were quite indifferent concerning the welfare of their cat. She was left to shift for herself. It was some time before we discovered that she too had a family. The burden was too heavy, so she had come to us for help. She was so nearly starved that we did not have the heart to turn her away.

For several days she came every morning to get her pan of milk. It was fully a week before she made it known that she had decided to stay. By that time she had won the mistress of the house by her unusual show of gratitude. She would not touch the food that was given her until she had shown her appreciation by rubbing the hand that fed her.

Betty's family of four were about half grown before they were discovered. Unknown to us, she had carried them nearly a mile from her old home and hidden them under an outbuilding. I had seen her carrying a mouse or a gopher under there several times, but had suspected nothing. There had not been a squeak out of those kittens until their mother was satisfied that they were old enough to take care of themselves. She was taking no chances.

The cat problem was now a real one; homes for the surplus were not easy to find. There was no cause for joy, therefore, when Betty gave evidence of her second family. She had not been granted the same privileges that Puff had, but she would slip into the house when she could. One morning she was discovered in my wife's room. She had failed to get her tail out of sight when she crawled under the quilt at the foot of the bed. That had no doubt appealed to her as a fine place to have her babies. Of course she was put out. But an hour or so later she was found in a closet of the same room. This time she had selected a hatbox for a nursery. Once again she was ejected.

I was in the workshop that day, but had been informed of Betty's antics. My wife was going to town that afternoon, and she cautioned me not to let the cat into the house. Betty came into the workshop shortly after lunch. She had the run of the shop, of course. There was a box under the bench where I kept the shavings. I heard her rustling around in the box, but paid no attention to it. Perhaps an hour later I heard a noise coming from the box which prompted me to investigate.

Betty was vigorously washing the last of four babies. She looked up at me proudly, and gratefully. She had not felt it necessary to hide her kittens this time. And since I was her friend, she felt free to have them right under my nose. When the kittens were well grown, we managed to place them elsewhere —all but one.

That fellow was as black as the ace of spades, with long silky hair and big green eyes. He was as bright as a sunflower and always ready to play. He was not as affectionate as his mother, but he had her sense of gratitude. We named him Blackie, and he was truly a gorgeous cat.

He would follow me around the ranch like a dog. When I would be mowing the lawn, he would hop up on my shoulder and run his rough tongue over my cheek. There had been a time when I would have annihilated a cat for taking such liberties. But this was Blackie! He probably knew he owed his life to me. Had his mother not told him so? He never tired of showing his gratitude.

Betty's Vigil

BETTY HAD BEEN WITH US FOR SOME two years when our horse Lady took sick. She was a very inquisitive cat, constantly investigating things about the ranch. The animals all seemed to like her. Even the chickens had no fear of her. She had a way with her.

We had worked with the sick horse most of that day. I had noticed that Betty was close by most of the time, but had paid little attention to her, putting it down to her intense curiosity.

Before retiring that night I went to the corral to have a look at the horse. Somewhat to my surprise, I found Betty lying close beside the sick animal. She kept rubbing against me as I examined the horse. She was probably trying to tell me that she understood. When I left the barn I fully expected her to follow me to the house, but she did not. She stayed with the horse.

I made a second visit to the barn around two or three o'clock in the morning. Betty was still there. She was doing her best, no doubt, to comfort her sick friend. When I went again at feeding time, the horse was dead. Betty was sitting a few feet from Lady's head, watching with very sad eyes. She knew her friend was gone, and it was plainly evident that she was deeply grieved.

Spot Shows Her Displeasure

ONE OF THE FIRST THINGS I LEARNED about cats was that they have a very forceful way of showing their feelings at times. There had always been a cat about the place, and at this particular time it was a big black and white female. Spot was her name.

This cat rarely came to the house; her home was in the barn. Now and then she would come to the kitchen door for a pan of milk; otherwise she subsisted on rats. The barn had about outlived its usefulness, so it was replaced by a new structure. Spot watched the destruction of her old home with evident perplexity. She never so much as glanced at the rats as they scurried to other quarters. And when the wrecking was completed, Spot had disappeared.

No one shared my belief that she had left home to show her disapproval. No, something must have happened to her. Some three months later, however, she returned. Certainly nothing had happened to her, she was as fat as ever, with not a hair out of place.

Spot took possession of a small building which had not been used for some time. I had never seen any rats in it, but Spot thrived nevertheless. The following year we decided to eliminate this building also. And once again that cat disappeared. It was at least two months before she returned.

I was in the workshop at the time. It was late fall, and quite cold. I heard a cat outside, but was too much interested in my work to give it any thought. Presently I looked up to see Spot sitting on the window sill. I spoke to her, and she answered with a switch of her tail. She was at the door when I opened it. She immediately curled up by the stove and went to sleep.

Now, this was the cat that would never come in the house. I did a little pondering as I went about my work, and I was not long in deciding that Spot was deserving of more consideration than she had been given heretofore. If she would accept of my hospitality, I would share the workshop with her. I cut a small opening in one corner of the wall so that she might come and go as she pleased. A bed was also fixed for her under the bench.

Spot was perfectly contented with that arrangement, and that was her home for the balance of her days.

It was quite evident that Spot felt that she was entitled to a home of her own. When those she had chosen were demolished, she knew of no way of expressing her disapproval except by leaving home.

Instinct versus Desire

MANY YEARS' EXPERIENCE WITH animals has convinced me that, by and large, our silent friends have a deep-seated desire to please us. But too often they are denied the opportunity to prove it. We believe the following incident should illustrate the strength of this desire.

When we bought our home in the mountains, we inherited two Persian kittens. They had been born the day we first looked at the property. We named the male Happy, the female Gay. For quite some time it looked as if Happy would be quite a problem. He was a lovable bundle of fur, but he had a marked streak of selfishness in his makeup; also a determination to have his own way at all times.

Denial of cherished privileges, however, eventually convinced him that obedience was a virtue well worth cultivating. And in time it became evident that he was really trying to please, as best he knew.

One day, while my wife and I were sitting in the living room, a bird flew against one of the windows. We could see it fall, and when we reached the window it was laying motionless on the ground. And less than a yard away Happy was crouching, ready to spring upon it. My wife tapped on the window and said, "No, no, Happy." I rushed out of the house to rescue the bird, somewhat surprised to find that Happy had not moved. I patted him, and gave him due praise before taking the bird inside.

We found the little fellow was only stunned. He soon revived and was set free. Now, it is quite natural for a cat to consider any member of the bird family fair prey. That is simple instinct. But, to us at least, Happy had demonstrated that his desire to please his folks was even stronger than instinct.

Happy Listens

IT IS INTERESTING TO OBSERVE THE WAY in which an intelligent animal accumulates his store of knowledge in the complex world of man. Strangely enough, he appears to be less confused than man himself. This incident is offered as an illustration of his adaptability.

A cat may easily deceive us regarding his capacity for knowledge, so much of the time he appears quite indifferent to what goes on about him. But that does not mean that he has failed to observe.

As a rule our cats were not allowed into the house, except at feeding time, or by the fireside during winter evenings. They had sleeping quarters in the garage but were always fed in the kitchen. Of course, they would slip out of the kitchen any time an opportunity presented itself.

Happy was the one that knew how to open the door to the living room. He had learned that by hooking his claws on the edge of the door he could pull it open. That was possible, however, only when the door had failed to latch, as it often did if not carefully closed.

The interesting part of it was that Happy knew when that door was latched and when it was not. There was a difference in the click of the latch, and he had learned what that difference meant. If the latch had caught, he made no move. If it had not, he was at the door instantly to pry it open. Happy's ears had told him all he needed to know.

Fireside Peace

ALL ANIMALS ARE EXTREMELY SENSITIVE to their surroundings. They are at their best in an atmosphere of quiet harmony. Our dog Tippy exemplified this to a marked degree.

There was much confusion in this dog's first home because of several rather rowdy youngsters. Nor was harmony a part of the home life. This condition was plainly reflected in the dog's attitude as well as in his expression. He was loyal and faithful to his family, even to saving the baby from drowning when he was only a year old. But he was not a happy dog.

Tippy's attitude changed almost immediately when he found himself a part of our family circle. He seemed to realize that he was no longer looked upon as only a dog. He was a definite and important member of his new family. And he responded accordingly.

Tippy's transformation was complete. Within a few months it was difficult to believe he was the same dog we had first seen. Unsuspected characteristics came to the surface, all developed by a more congenial atmosphere.

When the animals were permitted to join the family on a winter evening, each had a definite place by the fireside. Tippy did not like much heat, so his place was on a blanket at one side, near my favorite chair. The cats took their places on the hassocks that flanked the fireplace. There they would spend an entire evening in perfect contentment. A better-behaved family could hardly have been found.

Should we have callers, however, that peaceful scene was instantly changed. Tippy would give the alarm, of course, and the cats would disappear under the couch. Should the callers be of those few whom the cats had accepted, they would resume their places and settle down again. Otherwise they would not show themselves, unless to slip over to the door and ask to be let out. They resented having their peace disturbed by strangers.

Two men came to see me one blustery afternoon. They were wearing work clothes, and one of them elected to sit on Happy's hassock close to the fire. That evening when the cats came in, Happy refused to take his accustomed seat. He sniffed at the hassock—and turned up his nose probably, although I could not observe that. Casting a disapproving glance at his mistress, he stretched out upon the hearth. Nothing would induce him to take his rightful place.

It was my understanding mate who sensed the cause of Happy's conduct. Procuring soap and water, she gave that leather hassock a thorough scrubbing. Happy watched her curiously. When she had finished, he got up and sniffed at it again very carefully. Apparently satisfied, he hopped up and was soon sleeping quite contentedly.

Our caller of the afternoon had evidently left an odor on the seat he had occupied. We could not detect it, but Happy had. And to him it was offensive. He did not propose having his tranquillity disturbed by any unsavory odors.

Fowls

Colorful and useful,
even these lack not wisdom

An Appeal for Help

one of the most stupid creatures that walks. That opinion, however, has little foundation. In fact, it is a grave injustice to that noble bird. The following incidents may help to correct such an opinion.

The thieving coyotes were always our worst problem in raising turkeys on the ranch. By nature the turkey is a rover, thriving best when he can forage at will. He abhors confinement; hence he is an easy prey for the crafty coyote.

The turkey hens seldom went far to make their nests, but as soon as the young were able to travel, one never knew where they were. One of our hens, however, demonstrated that she knew better. She had made her nest not far from the house, and she never took her babies beyond what she must have considered a safe distance.

This hen was a great pet, coming to the house every day to have someone talk to her and make a fuss over her. She had been given a coop near the pump house, where she could roam over a six-acre field. She never left the field, except to bring her brood to the house to show them off. She was very proud of her babies.

They liked it around the house and, if they had been allowed, would probably have stayed there. The grass was tempting, and the flowerbeds provided a good supply of bugs. But that was a privilege we had to deny them. Only twice was it necessary to drive them back to the field. After that it was only necessary to give them due recognition and tell the mother to take her babies back where they belonged. She certainly understood, for that was exactly what she would do. Off she would go, calling her babies to follow. That performance might be repeated two or three times each day.

One morning I saw them coming to the house much earlier than usual, and apparently they were in a great hurry. There was no stopping on the way to catch an unwary insect; straight to the house they came. In fact, they came right up onto the front porch. That was something they had never done before. This was going a little too far, so I drove them off, scolding the mother for teaching her babies bad tricks.

They left the porch under vigorous protest. Their actions were so peculiar that I was puzzled. The youngsters were not permitted to explore the flowerbeds this morning. Mother hen kept them close to her with a constant chatter.

There was a low hill about a hundred yards from the house. That hen kept looking up at the hill with a *pirt, pirt,* in a tone I had never heard her use before. I knew she was trying to tell me something, but I couldn't get it. She was nervous, evidently quite disturbed about something. Since there was nothing visible that might have caused her alarm, I made a fuss over her and told her to take her babies back home. She did so, but very reluctantly.

But it was not long before she was back again, and this time it was necessary to drive her out of the yard. She kept that up most of the day; yet we saw nothing to account for her disturbance.

It was our custom to shut the turkeys in their coops before dark. Then they would be safe for the night, at least. This particular evening we were having dinner with one of our neighbors. Mother and her brood were out on their last forage of the day when it was time for us to leave. Thinking we would probably be back before dark, I was not concerned about them.

It was rather late, however, before we returned. The first thing I did was to lock the doors of the turkey coops. It was dark, of course, and it never occurred to me to check up on them. I just took it for granted that all was well.

Imagine my feelings when I went to feed in the morning. The coop at the pump house was deserted. The babies were foraging not far off, but there was no sign of their mother. About a hundred feet from the coop I found the answer to the mystery of the day before. Mother turkey's feathers were mute evidence of the night's tragedy.

Probably we had not been long gone that evening before the watchful coyote had come off the hill. It was clear that there had been a battle. The mother had saved her children, at the cost of her own life. The thieving coyote had very likely been watching those turkeys all day, and the mother knew it. Our pet had done her utmost to tell us of the danger. She had brought her family to the house, begging for protection. But we were too dense to understand.

Tom Takes Charge

had been an isolated case, some doubt might remain regarding the question of intelligence. It was not, however. In fact, it was closely followed by another almost as interesting, and in some respects even more remarkable.

It is well known that, above all things, a male turkey is a show-off. He spends most of his time strutting. He is truly the king of the barnyard, and he knows it. He never loses an opportunity to display his superiority. He takes no part in the rearing of his family and has little patience for his homely children.

The death of mother turkey posed a problem. Her babies were not old enough to shift for themselves; coyotes would have picked them off in no time. There was no place to confine them, even had that been advisable. We put their coop in the back yard not far from the kitchen. This would permit someone to keep an eye on them most of the time. There was no telling what the king might do if they wandered into the corral. Gobblers had been known to kill their offspring, but we had to take that chance.

The youngsters had hardly been settled in their new location when Tom appeared on the scene. Naturally, he was watched with considerable suspicion. But his actions quickly proved that there was no cause for concern. As far as he was able he took over the parental duties where the mother had left off. He herded those babies in grand style, talking to them and directing them to choice edibles. He would leave them at intervals while he returned to his bailiwick to display his glory, but he was never gone long.

Every evening Tom would accompany the babies on a final forage, then herd them into the coop. He would then strut off

to his roost, as much as to say, "I've done my duty for the day." When they were large enough, he took them to roost with him on the corral fence.

It was quite evident that Tom understood the situation. He must have known what had happened to the babies' mother. So he had smothered his pride and assumed the responsibilities of a parent. It was also plain to be seen that he was decidedly proud of his success.

Tom Co-operates

IT MIGHT BE WELL TO CITE ONE MORE incident before coming to any conclusion regarding the question of intelligence—that is so far as it affects the turkey family.

At another time we had a very fine tom turkey, a bronze weighing nearly forty pounds. He spent most of his time around the corral, displaying his gorgeous plumage for the benefit of his small world. The horses always had access to the corral day and night. Sometimes there would be considerable confusion when things happened not to go smoothly. At such times Tom always managed to slip indifferently to a place of safety. He showed no fear of the animals, but he took no chances on having his beauty marred.

One day he was found under a feed box with a broken leg. How it had happened no one knew. He had probably been caught in a stampede. The first thought, of course, was that he would have to be killed. That would be my job, and I didn't fancy it. Tom was an old friend. I would talk to him, and no matter how busy he might be he never failed to answer me with his merry gobble.

It seemed rather foolish to try repairing that broken leg, but I decided it was worth the effort. I took him into the barn, set the broken bone, and put a stout splint on it. Tom made no protest, never once attempting to escape. Then I shut him in a small chickenhouse that was not being used at the time. He ate his supper balancing himself on one leg.

Instinct urges the turkey to seek the highest roosting place as a matter of safety. Therefore, just before dark I put Tom up on the roost. I knew that, if I removed the perch, he would be fretting to get to his old roost. Allowing his injured leg to hang free, he settled down in apparent contentment.

He was still there, standing on one leg, when I went to feed him in the morning. He seemed so well satisfied where he was that I fed him out of my hand. And that was where he spent the day. Satisfied by this time that he understood what was required of him, I arranged feed and water where he could help himself without leaving the perch.

Tom never left that perch for two full weeks. He would greet me with a low gobble when I went to see him; otherwise there was not a sound from him. It was as though he did not want it known that he was in confinement.

At the end of the two weeks I removed the splint. His leg was completely healed. Tom looked at it, then at me as much as to say, "I'm afraid to take a chance." So I lifted him to the floor. Very gingerly, he tested the injured leg. And when he found it would support his weight, he gave expression to his joy in a voice that could be heard all over the place. I opened the door and out he went, strutting his splendor with great gusto. Needless to say, when Tom died it was of old age.

Human Beings Preferred

TO MOST PEOPLE, A CHICKEN IS JUST A chicken. Quite useful, of course, but of no particular interest, not even to its owner. To the casual observer, a flock of hens will look as much alike as peas in a pod. Close observation, however, will reveal the fact that they too possess individual characteristics. Often these characteristics will prove decidedly interesting, and well worth developing, if one will take the time.

This was shown quite forcibly with an Ancona hen we once owned. She was so unusual that we felt she deserved a name, so we called her Ana. She was one of a small flock of chicks raised in a brooder. When only a few days old, she gave evidence of her individuality. She was more alert, more independent, and far more friendly than was common. She would hop on one's hand and sit there as long as anyone cared to pet her.

This chick showed a definite fondness for her human friends, and the attachment grew stronger as she grew older. No fence was high enough to keep Ana in confinement; she came and went as she pleased. When a chicken manages to escape from its confinement, it never seems able to find the way back again. That might indicate that they have no memory, but Ana disproved that. She might fly over the fence a dozen times a day, but she would always fly back again when she so desired.

She never failed to come to the house each morning. She would set up a loud chatter until someone went out to bid her good morning. After having been petted to her satisfaction, she would go off in search of a bug, merrily singing her contentment.

There was no question about this feathered mite having a real craving for human affection. And her appreciation was just as marked. That was shown clearly enough in her responsive gestures, her merry chatter. The companionship of her own kind did not satisfy this independent bird. And she had the intelligence to know how she could obtain what she craved. Ana was a little more than just a chicken—at least she was decidedly individual.

Santee the Showman

WE SENT A STRING OF BLACK MINORCAS to the show in the southern part of the state one winter. The day before the birds were to be shipped, the cock that had been selected developed a cold.

There was only one other good enough for exhibition. He was really the finest bird of the flock, but as a cockerel he had shown a white feather in one wing. Since that disqualified him for exhibition, I had not looked him over for some time. When I did examine him, I was surprised to find that his wing had moulted out in perfect color. He was shipped to the show, but there was no reason to expect much of him, for the reason that he had not been handled.

It usually requires weeks of careful handling to train a bird for the show. Untrained, a bird is not likely to behave very well in strange surroundings. The chances are that it will crowd into a corner when the judge comes along, making it difficult to see the bird's good points.

This particular bird so closely resembled a blue-ribbon winner I had seen at Madison Square Garden many years before that I named him for the owner. At that time Dr. Santee was the country's foremost breeder of the Black Minorcas.

Well, our Santee turned out to be a perfect show bird,

regardless of the fact that he had not been trained. He was up on his toes, showing to the best advantage when the judge came to look at him. Shortly afterward, a blue ribbon was fastened to Santee's cage. And that bird actually seemed to know what it meant. He was as proud as a peacock.

The judge was so impressed with Santee that he had him placed in a turkey coop where he would show to better advantage. Weighing nearly eleven pounds, he was a big bird in every way. Even the turkey cage was none too large for him.

Santee won every prize within his reach, including grand champion of the show. His ribbons were all blue ones, and did he strut! He would sit down and rest when he had a chance, but the minute anyone came to look at him he was up again to display himself with great pride.

Was that because his ancestors had been in the show business for so many generations? Had it come down through the years to Santee? We will never know, of course. I only know that I never owned a more perfect show bird—and without a moment's training.

Spoiled

OUR PRIZE HEN TOOK SICK ON THE WAY home from that same show. She would not eat for days. When she finally did take a little interest in food, it was only when I fed her by hand. Inasmuch as she was one of our best breeders, I humored her.

She finally recovered from her illness, and I put her back

with the flock. But would that hen scratch for her grain, as she always had before? She would not. She had evidently discovered something during her stay in the hospital. She would look up at me as much as to say, "Okay, I'm waiting to be served."

She would eat dry mash from the hopper; she didn't have to stoop for that. But as long as she lived she would pick nothing from the floor or from the ground outside. She was so amusing that I continued to feed her by hand.

Had her success at the show gone to her head? No, hardly that. It was more likely because she had cultivated a liking for the easier way. And she was clever enough to get away with it.

The Inspector

WE HAD ONE LARGE HOUSE ON THE ranch where we kept about a hundred laying hens. It was a custom to clean the dropping boards every morning. I had long since learned that hens were happier in clean quarters. Cleanliness contributes to health, and health is equally important to happiness. And, in my humble opinion, happiness is the secret of success in the handling of our silent friends.

There was one hen in this particular flock that took to hopping up on the platform when I would be cleaning it. She had no fear. The noise of the metal scraper did not disturb her in the least. She would follow it with her bright little eyes as it went back and forth. Then she would come to the edge of the platform to peer curiously into the box where the droppings were being scraped.

There was no mistaking her, because of a peculiar mark on her comb. It was always the same bird. And she never missed a day, unless she happened to be on the nest at the time.

Was this hen merely curious? If so, one would have thought her curiosity would have been satisfied after a while. Or did she somehow consider it her duty to see that the job was properly done?

Random Sketches

Whether they soar through the air, or roam the forest;
whether they live under the ground, or crawl on their bellies:
They were all created by the Great Architect
with a definite place and purpose
in the Divine Plan

The Lazy Centipede

I ONCE CAPTURED A VERY FINE SPECIMEN
of the centipede family. It was the largest one I had ever seen,
and I intended to preserve it.

I put it in a glass jar and took it to the house, with the idea
of studying its habits for a few days. It was soon discovered that
the moth was this fellow's favorite article of food. Moths were
plentiful, so he was given all he could eat. They must have been
a rare delicacy, for there was nothing left but dust when he had
finished with them.

Somehow he escaped. Of course, no one knew anything
about it, but it was certain that he had been given assistance.
He had tried to get out of the jar at first, but the smooth glass
was too much for him. Then, when he found that there was
always plenty for him to eat, he made no further effort to escape.
He appeared to be perfectly contented.

The day following the centipede's escape I saw him out on
the lawn. At least, I was rather certain it was the same one,
because of his size. I immediately went for the jar in which he
had spent about a week. I made no attempt to catch him this
time. I merely placed the jar on the ground about two feet ahead
of him, directly in line of his progress.

He stopped when some three or four inches from the jar. His feelers became very active, and I fully expected him to change his course. Instead, he walked right into that jar without the slightest hesitation. I did not touch the jar for several minutes. I was waiting for him to discover his mistake. But no, he settled down as though he were perfectly satisfied.

Unquestionably he had been ejected from his new home. It looked as though he had not been happy about it. Hunting for his provisions probably no longer appealed to him. He knew where he could feed better without stirring himself. Perhaps he too, like the Minorca hen, had a weakness for the softer way of life.

Pete Lays an Egg

ONE SPRING OUR NEAREST NEIGHBOR found a baby dove on the hillside near his house. It had fallen out of a nest and was not old enough to fly. The nest was empty, and there was no sign of the parents. Therefore, he took the little fellow home. He fed it with a dropper until it was old enough to eat bread crumbs. He named the bird Pete.

Pete's bed was on top of the water heater in the kitchen. That was where he spent the nights, but during the day he was unrestricted. He came and went as he pleased. He delighted in riding around on his master's shoulder, chattering to him all the while.

Pete often came to call on us. He liked the workshop, if I were working there. He would strut up and down the bench chattering to me or rustle in the shavings. He took to hopping up on a shelf above the bench, where he could watch me.

He flew in the shop one afternoon with a great chatter. He alighted on the shelf and disappeared. I heard him scratching up there but paid no attention to him. Finally, after being very quiet for some time, he appeared on the edge of the shelf. He tried to tell me something before he left, but I didn't understand the language.

When curiosity finally prompted me to take a look, I discovered that the bird had been given the wrong name. Pete had laid an egg.

Pete had many visitors that fall when the winter migration began. The doves were trying to induce him—or her—to join them on their southern jaunt. Finally she did join one flock, and we were certain we had seen the last of that bird. But we were wrong; Pete was back the next afternoon.

Evidently one night away from home had been enough for Pete. That bird was not accustomed to sleeping in the open. The cozy bed in the kitchen was more to her liking. Anyway, Pete never left home again.

The Blue and the Gray

BEING IN THE HEART OF THE FOREST, our place was well populated by citizens of the other world. Birds and squirrels were especially numerous. We put up a cafeteria not far from the house to encourage these beautiful children of nature to come close enough for us to enjoy them.

It was a joy indeed to watch the blue jays when the snow came. With their trim little bodies dressed in blue, and their cocky black crests, they made a lovely picture against the glistening white background.

There was a family of four gray squirrels that made good use of the cafeteria. One of them rarely missed a day. The others were more infrequent callers. This one became rather friendly after a while. He was easily identified, and we named him Greedy.

This fellow had an amazing capacity for peanuts. He would stuff himself first. Then, if there were any nuts left, he would take them home to the family, or bury them close by. It was most interesting to watch him cache those nuts for future need. When he had covered the holes with pine needles, an Indian would more than likely have had trouble locating them.

If the cupboard happened to be bare when Greedy called, he would certainly let us know about it. He would scamper up a near-by tree and chatter in a scolding tone until someone produced more nuts.

The blue jay family was quite a large one. There must have been twenty that made use of the cafeteria. There was one vociferous fellow that seemed to be the leader. Anyway, he was the spokesman of the clan.

When the supply of grain became exhausted, he too knew how to notify us. My workshop was not far from the cafeteria and had several trees in front of it. If I happened to be in the workshop, this bird would fly into the nearest tree and start to scold. He could see me through the window, and he would not let up until I had produced more feed.

These fellows did not hesitate to take full advantage of our hospitality. They seemed to think it was due them. And it really was, for they added much to the colorful atmosphere of our home.

The Yellow Jackets

THE INTELLIGENCE OF THE HONEYBEE
can hardly be questioned. Those industrious little fellows have a highly organized and strictly disciplined society that would seem to leave little room for doubt on that score.

But what of the other members of that winged family of insects, those pugnacious species that are so generally feared? Are they without intelligence? The following is given merely to provoke thought upon the question, not to answer it.

When we drilled a well on the ranch, I built a small house over it as quickly as possible to protect the equipment from the elements. It was finished on the outside, but not on the inside until several weeks later. The door, or a window, was always left open for ventilation.

It was not long before I discovered that a family of yellow jackets were building a new home in the pump house. I couldn't blame them, for it looked like an ideal location for them. I was in and out of that building nearly every day, but paid no attention to the uninvited tenants. Nor did they seem at all concerned about my comings and goings.

When I finally found time to finish the building, the yellow jackets had completed their home. I worked inside the small building for two days. I did not disturb their cleverly built home but worked around it as best I could. I drove nails within a foot of that busy cluster of bees; yet they never appeared unduly disturbed. Some of them would alight on my hat, my shoulders, or even on my hands for a quick inspection. Not once did they touch my face. They certainly had reason to be concerned about my noisy presence, yet they did not appear to be. I just talked to them and went on with my work. Not once did they offer to sting me.

It was decidedly unhealthy, however, for a stranger to enter that building. The yellow jackets demonstrated that on more than one occasion. They had apparently accepted me as a friend, but they were taking no chances with strangers.

This may be no proof of intelligence on the part of those insects, but it would appear to indicate that even those seemingly insignificant citizens are not without their quota of understanding. Yet, why should there be any doubt of it; were they not created by the one Supreme Intelligence?

FRIENDS OF MINE

To all those friends of mine
    In simple truth I can say,
I am indeed most grateful
    For many, many a happy day.

So very much that is good
    Those friends have shown.
Yes, but for them indeed
    Much I might have never known.

Never caring what I owned,
    What might my family be,
Quite satisfied were they
    To love, to serve just me.

Never critical, nor complaining,
    Those faithful friends of mine;
No great friendship feigning.
    Silent friends, but, oh, so fine.
                E. S. H.

www.ingramcontent.com/pod-product-compliance
Lightning Source LLC
Chambersburg PA
CBHW030528260626
47157CB00005B/1924